STET

PETER READING

Stet

Secker & Warburg
London

First published in England 1986 by
Martin Secker & Warburg Limited
54 Poland Street, London W1V 3DF

Reprinted 1986

British Library Cataloguing in Publication Data

Reading, Peter
Stet.
I. Title
821'.914   PR6068.E27
ISBN 0–436–40989–5

Typeset by Inforum Ltd, Portsmouth
Printed in England by
Redwood Burn Ltd, Trowbridge

Pyrex, a pie-dish, deep-lined with apple lumps,
deft in the left hand; with the right, flopping on
pall of white-dusted droopy pastry,
slicing off overlaps, jabbing steam-vents . . .

'52: Mummy paused, wiped a floured hand and tuned in the wireless –
sad Elgar, crackling, then *death of our King, George the Sixth.*

'Wrote to Miss Prudence, you know at *Comfy Home*
"Time will heal all wounds wonderful" *she* says
"No need to av flowers nless yer wants em.
        Yer can wear black if yer wants to" *she* says.'

Engines cut out, thick snow dumbed harmonious
doves numbed in frozen postures of flight and we
found in the eerie too-bright morning
        rhubarb leaves crusting the ice-whorled window.

Those at the bank and the grocer's are that peculiar fetial
brand of perniciousness which wars and cold climates produce.

Muse!, sing the Grotty [scant alternative].

Cro-Magnon, simian, Neanderthal,
whom Mr Justice Russell sentences
to 46 years (total) for assault
on Mr Harry Tipple and his wife . . .

Charles Bradford, Terence Bradford, Edward Mitchell,
broke into Mr Tipple's corner shop.
After they had assaulted him he had
black eyes, a broken nose, bruised lacerated
torso and face and buttocks. He had his head
banged on the floor and had his feet stamped on.
He was knocked senseless with a bottle. Cans
of aerosol paint and fly-spray were fizzed up
his nose and mouth. Bradford and Mitchell next
started to cut his ear off, but then hacked
off Tipple's toe with a serrated knife.
The toe was then stuffed into Tipple's mouth
(playing *This Little Piggy* on the kid's
little pink blobs is not so much fun now).

And Mrs Tipple croodles in the box
as she explains how both her eyes were blacked,
her nose was broken, she was 'in the most
humiliating and degrading way'
indecently assaulted by the men –
one of whom 'used a knife in an obscene
bizarre vile filthy ithyphallic manner'.
Charles Bradford, Terence Bradford, Edward Mitchell,
before they left the Tipples bound and gagged,
turned, faced them, and, unzipping, each produced
his member and pissed long and copiously
into the faces of the hapless pair.

An acned trio lowers from the front page.
Cro-Magnon, simian, Neanderthal
(but the same species as Christ, Einstein, Bach).

[Trite impotent iambic journalese,
Reading Raps Raiders/Poet Pete Protests.]

[Re-draft the sick obsessional chuntering,
     strike out the old gratuitous cruelties . . .
          (re-draft be buggered, leave as printed,
               Hail!, uncorrectable Age of Floored Proofs).]

When (early '60s?) there was an influx of
     collared doves spreading rapidly through the realm,
          monthly we mapped the species' progress
               (hanging for murder was being phased out –

noosed necks diminished/proliferated in inverse ratio),
     dubbed it the Year of the Noose; unforeseen increase ensued.

Obsolete bivalves of the Silurian
     scutter from flaked rock onto a Viva squashed
          in the Scrap Merchant's disused quarry
               (lugged in on Saturday – bad do, A5).

We went to see it that evening; bashed-in badly, the near-side.
     Mangled up into the roof, strands of maroon-stained blonde hair.

and it is these hydrogen atoms' radio emissions to which I refer. The wavelength at which hydrogen atoms radiate is, of course, 21.106 centimetres, and when I tune the scope to this wavelength, what I am able to record is static hydrogen – neither moving towards nor away from us.

And if you wish to 'observe' advancing or retreating clouds containing this interstellar gas?

Well, if I re-tune to 21.105 centimetres, then I am able to record clouds that are moving towards us at a velocity of 50 000 kilometres per hour. If I retune to 21.107 centimetres, then I am able to record clouds which are moving away at the same velocity.

This 'Hydrogen Line' was predicted, was it not, by Hendrick van de Hulst, the Dutch astronomer, during the war, and first detected in 1951?

Correct. And, of course, there are other radio emissions from other materials in space, detectable at different wavelengths – for example, the first molecule found in space by my colleague in 1963, a water molecule minus one hydrogen atom, (OH), hydroxyl, radiates at a wavelength of 18 centimetres. But most molecules radiate at the shorter, often submillimetre, wavelengths bordering on the far infrared.

And what of your own particular concerns?

Yes, well, I've no interest whatsoever in our local system, in isolation. My concern is the very furthest reaches, where the colossal explosions of the quasars are faintly

[Bellicose *H. sap.*] Skull-cleaving Harriers,
distant a field before their ventriloquous
stridencies strip dense gold male flowers,
hedge-hop me pruning the *Quercus ilex*.

Valorous, some of them, homicides all by grey acquiescence.
Holm sap is smeared and it smells bitterly on the poised blade.

'53: gleeful, briskly we marched from the
Infants to see the New Coronation and
Everest Conquered, double feature,
into a gaudily faded *Regal*.

Tenzing and Hillary flickering, last real British achievement/
shock of the shot of our new Monarch sat *twiddling its thumbs!*

When the daft queen came to Bootle the crowd stank sweat-rank and
squashed me;
scuffers controlled it – I liked [still do] Law more than the Mob.

I thank you kindly sir! Bitter and mild mixed.
Like I was saying like, once they gets in like,
you know to Parlerment, hear no more of em.
Taxes and that like and where's it all going?
Not to the pensioners any road, mister.
Same with the kids in the schools an that now see,
parents has got to ave whip-rounds and that like –
pay for the stuff as the kids use in school like.
Course when the Goverment sees as it's able
not to spend taxes on kids' educations,
they cuts the school money more see – they knows like
how the old parents'll have a whip-round like.
Same with the Health Service money and that like,
Goverment knows as the public'll whip-round
so as to get what the hospitals need like.
That's what the Goverment wants cos the private
patients is all right and others has whip-rounds –
pay for the hospital stuff as is needed.
Therefore the Goverment don't have to pay for
schools and the Health Service so there's more tax for nucular
                                              warflair.

Probably merely twinge of dyspepsia,
    nothing at all, just tremulous tightness to
        left of the sternum, absolutely
            peak of condition and body tip-top,

stick to the Perrier more in the future, high fibre diet,
    jogging, longevity, yes, jogging, longevity, yes.

Esther Albouy was twenty-one years old
when the war ended, and she was denounced,
by neighbours in her village in the Auvergne,
for fraternizing with a German soldier.
She had her head shaved in the Public Square.
Her parents, who were overcome with shame,
then locked her in her room, letting her out
only at night, occasionally, on a leash.
When, after twenty years, her parents died,
she could not bear to face the outside world.
No one had seen her go outside the house
for thirty-eight years.

1983:
some Carmelite nuns managed, at last, to get
an eviction order for a house they owned
where no rent had been paid for many years
by the occupants – an old woman recluse
and her two brothers.

The *Gendarmerie*
had to use gas-masks when they forced their way
into the house, so overpowering was
the stench from filth and a green rotting corpse
(one of the brothers died three years before).
The gas and water had been long cut off.

She and her one surviving brother, whom
she slept in the same bed with, were removed
into a psychiatric hospital,
tenir en laisse, so she is pleased to think.

[Strike out the old obsessional nastiness,
justify, take out all the extraneous,
    PRINTER, insert rule, take back, wrong fount,
        change damaged character(s), strike out error . . .]

La bouche amère, cru gâté, sécheresse.

My sole concern is unmoving hydrogen
(Hydrogen Line predicted by van de Hulst)
    bunched between distant stellar clusters,
        tuned into 21.106 . . .
        [Let it stand; Reasonless causal physics.]

['McDonald (Mrs), Aberdeen' is adjudged
winner of Poem of the Week.]

Dirty sex violence of TV
    Should never be allowed
No wonder we can see
    The badly-behaved crowd!
Och! They will be punished
    On the Judgement Day,
Before the Lord is finished
    They will rue the day!
These do-gooder social workers
    Saying 'Let them go free'
Are all sinful shirkers
    Sent by Satan 'gainst you and me.
The way to stop these hooglums
    At football match or fight
Is string them up by thumbs
    Until they can tell Right
From Wrong, then ways of Jesus
    Will get into their heart
Which, at the present, freezes
    And they know not where Love starts.

'Gie im a pint quick – diggin is grave wi is
prick e is, this bloke: seen im on Satdy night
    parked in the Quarry, winders steamed-up,
        flattened them oats o mine, randy fuckerrr.'

A bloke with whom I once worked at the mill,
one bait-time, in the Bait-Room, peeled the lid
back from his Tupper sandwich-box, produced
two off-white thick amorphous slabs of bread
wherefrom a pinkish greyish matter oozed.
He bit, considered, rolled blear red-veined eyes,
spat an envenomed mouthful on the floor,
hurled the offending bait-box to his feet
(Terpsichoreans might have found the way
he rain-danced it to smithereens beneath
steel-toe-capped boots inspired, original),
then opined 'Fucking stupid bloody cow!
Wait till I get the bitch; I'll give her *jam
over beef dripping!*' Next day he was off.
They did him (GBH?). She had to have
23 stitches – he was a big bloke.
One time, he'd been all day and half the night
hard on the piss (the Vaults and then the Club),
and on the way home stumbled against a white
new-painted door. Dismayed, he bought some meths
down at the late-night Chemist. In the house,
he dabbed his jacket liberally and then
fell asleep on the sofa. When his wife
came back from visiting her sister, she
found him in drunk repose reeking of meths,
the emptied bottle lying at his side.
She beat him with a heavy casserole-
dish (which had been a wedding present from
her mother, twenty-three long years before)
until the blood streamed. Some ententes rely
much on a reciprocity of malice.

Killed the apprentice – *would* do, a tractor tyre.
Somehow he read the pressure-gauge faultily,
kept on inflating with the air-hose.
Sounded like dynamite. Split right open.

Two decades' cobwebs were falling for nearly half an hour after;
sound-waves dislodged them – unveiled cross-members
gleaming like new.

[Don't go out there – you'll all catch your death of it,
sinister twits are in the ascendancy.
Plump up a stanza, close the brackets,
snuggle down into a cosy re-draft . . .]

{ Dogma-adherents,
{ Orthodox hirsutes, smug in eternal truth
learnt from absurd delusions of troglodytes
(*tantum religio potuit suadere malorum*) . . .
Heights of pernicious stupidity grow from molehills of nonsense.

I had been Crop Inspecting – C2 Pennal
which we'd provisionally bought as seed –
the eleven acres by the railway line,
and in that sheltered corner near the tunnel
someone, quite possibly in love, had been
lying. An Inter-City brayed two notes,
the Buffet car disgorged a Light Ale tin
into the especial, pseudo rural, scene:
holed Nuform, empty Long Life, laid-flat oats.

Headmaster's study: brass-knobbed Victorian
inlaid Morocco desk of mahogany,
    antimacassared leather armchair,
        waxy refulgence of polished volumes . . .

I was about 12, must have been '58,
when I was vouchsafed secular ecstasy
    (some misdemeanour, farting/Lord's Prayer) –
        suddenly, bruise-clouded winter evening

beamed an oblique shaft, apricot, genial,
through a grim dull pane onto the luminous
    Axminster, cheery, spring-piled spectrum,
        rendering misery worldly, nothing.

'Youth of today sir; never known punishment,
National Service, show em some discipline,
bring back the Birch or, like Iran has –
lectrical gedget to chop their hends orf!'

6000 acres, each hour, of rain forest
voguishly razed (at moment of going to
press) – the climactic consequences/
faunal extinctions are merely cosmic.

None of it matters except as an ego-chilling lacuna:
1.6 acres per sec . . . Fright = Ethical Zeal.

'3 Across: "Writer, not brave, wrote *Cavalcade*."
Tell you the truth I've only read two of his –
Portrait of Doreen Grey and that one
whatsit *The Trouble with Being Earnest*.'

Grans are bewildered by post-Coronation disintegration –
    offspring of offspring of *their* offspring infest and despoil.

'54: old Miss Clio was teaching us
[genuine name, 'Miss Clio' is, by the way]
    'There is no reason, is there, children,
        why you can't live with other little

children from other countries in happiness?
You are the ones whom we are depending on . . .'
    We have betrayed her, poor old Dodo –
        cleaving of crania, burnt-out Pandas . . .

This isn't Socrates, Einstein or Bach but just the same species
    bloodily on the front page kicking itself into mulch.

'55: comics (*better* class) offered us
Decent Types it was hoped we would emulate –
Shaftesbury, Gandhi, Dickens, Florence
Nightingale, Faraday, Curie, Elgar . . .

'85: some of us clearly have been more moved by the *worse* ones –
Bloody-Nosed Basher, The Yobbs, Sheik Fist The Middle East
Nit . . .

All in this place anticipate the Dreadful.

[The weak theatrical one-liner whine
before the scalpel. How to justify
expatiation? Call it a day at that.]

Bad dégustation; puant the cru, short, séché the finish.

At the 1985 Royal Naval Equipment Exhibition in Portsmouth, is a set of six gold-plated Sterling Mark IV submachine guns, each with 12 gold-plated 9mm bullets. Complete with magazine and bayonet, displayed in a walnut case, each costs £9,000. 'Ordered by a foreign construction company for Royalty', discloses the righteous (all those juicy jobs!) Sterling Co. of Dagenham, Essex.

Marvellous boost to British Economy . . .
thousands of jobs created in Armaments . . .
unemployed needy welcome new hope . . .
Export Achievement and can't you see that

had not Great Britain landed this wonderful
order for Saudi R.A.F. fighter planes,
[hordes of *Tornado* urbane zappers]
some other nation would soon have stepped in . . .

benefit to the needs of our own people . . .
Government not responsible . . . actions of
leaders of other . . . thus Great Britain's
Satrapess gloatingly self-applauding.

Another exhibit is a fast patrol vessel built by Souters of Cowes, Isle of Wight, for the Bahrain Navy.

Inside the 100ft vessel, the bridge roof is lined with grey suede and the public rooms smell of the fresh opulence of their cream leather seating.

Blue carpets cover the decks, and the best German furniture and equipment fills the galley.

The bathrooms are lined with royal blue marble, there is a sunken bath, the toilet bowls are of smoked glass, the taps are of 22 carat gold.

The master bedroom features an oval bed, the television and video rise from the floor and smoked glass mirrors line the walls. A Danish hi-fi system pipes music throughout.

A 20 millimetre gun and an anti-aircraft missile system are carried.

Accommodation for the crew of 15 is squashed into the forecastle, cramped bunks 18 inches apart.

The Bahrain Navy has paid £1.7 million for this Wasp class boat to be used by a 'very senior minister' of the tiny Gulf sheikdom.

'56: going home from the Juniors,
I read the headlines **Suez** and **Crisis Point** –
crikey! I thought, there must be something
terribly wrong with the nation's toilets;

soon if the Government didn't act there'd be all kinds of nasties
gushing up out of the drains, Britain would be [is] engulfed.

[The Editor is moved to publish *Not As Bad As All That* by 'Contented of. Telford, Mrs.']

I count my blessings every day
    And night before I go to bed,
A little 'Thank You' prayer I say
    On going to bed.
Because Our Lord has given me
    Two good strong legs and arms
I am not handicapped you see
    And eyesight to see His charms
Like the bright-coloured flowers
    And the bright blue of the sky
And Dame Nature's flowry bowers
    Quiet where I can lie.

This world is not as bad as all that
    In spite of the strikes and wars
And football violence and all that
    And mugging and 'Nature red in claw'.
So to Our Lord a praise I sing
    To thank Him for this life
That pleasures like a cup of tea can bring
    And my dear children and being a wife.

Fossil Silurian crinoids infest our cottage's walls of
    local stone; thin plasterboard separates them from ourselves.

Don't get me wrong now mate, just half in there thanks.
I thank you kindly sir! Don't get me wrong now.
I know we got to have army defences,
otherwise have bleeding lunatics step in,
then look out mister like that Ayertolly
you know or commies or some of them others –
all bleeding lunatics, L-O-N-U-T –
forcing the people to do what they say like.
That is Dictatorships, no-one wants that mate.
So there has got to be forces defences.
Mind you I don't say I holds with this bleeding
nucular warflair, don't hold with it me mate.
Too much of that bleeding lot an we all be
dead as a yo-yo mate. Bitter and mild please.
Same with them low-flying Harriers what they
trains off the Air-Base as deafens you almost
zoomin like that about twenty feet up like,
fetch all the blossom all off of the trees mate
with the vibration and that you know. They got
nucular bombs as they fires out of them mate.
Too much that nucular lot and we all be
dead as a yo-yo mate. Let it stand, I say. Dead as a yo-yo.

[Non-acquiescent acknowledgement; present but muted the
OIMOI!]

Very Long Baseline Interferometry
renders the quasar 3C 273
(2000 million light years distant)
clearly discernible – my sole interest . . .
[Stet; Ave!, Reasonless causal physics.]

Impasse of US/USSR has stopped
dangerous hate-states getting too uppity.
Volunteer acned cannon-fodder
(unemployed school-leavers, while supplies last)

keeps yellow oldies like me free from conscription. To these:
generous History, Geography, Stalemate, I am most grateful.

A lady's album of 1826
in my possession, contains the following
one-liner alexandrine unexplained:

Something ridiculous & sad will happen soon.

Top of the sequence: washer-shaped crinoid stalks/
brachiopods in layered Silurian
delvings of Wenlock Limestone quarry
disused except by the yokel neatherds

digging their graves with their pricks after late-night Saturday
piss-ups –
dark Vivas parked emit moans, Fetherlites pile up in shales.

'Sensitive things them Topical Rain Forests,
regulates all the Global Humility,
neccitates Nature Conversation,
otherwise animals Mass Distinction.'

Beadily, sloes still hang under midwinter
snow (a kind summer, autumn and freezing have
increased the fructose level somewhat),
sweeten a withering palate, slightly.

['Contented of Telford, Mrs.' submits her poem
Faith to the Editor.]

All this terrible rape and murder
    And mugging and violence galore
And poor little children beaten
    Oh! my heart can stand no more.
There is always someone on strike
    For better pay and terms,
Is there no end of this misery?
    No one ever learns.
But before despair descends
    Upon my sad head
A name crops up in the paper
    And I no longer wish I was dead!
I'm filled with fresh, new hope,
    I'm certain that Billy Graham,
With words of Truth and Love,
    Will bring an end to this horrid mayhem.

[Don't let the Old Ineluctable catch you with your clichés down –
    Cope with No Hope without god./Recognize, not acquiesce.]

When I was sacked from Uncle Chummy's Mail
(formerly Uncle Chummy's Letterbox)
for being tight – don't mind my telling you? –
I got the *Comfy Home*'s Miss Prudence page –
Problems and all that bilge, and Poetry.
'An incident occurred whereby some s * * * m
got in my mouth and then I swallowed it.
Can you get pregnant like this?' 'Do not fear,
my young friend, I enclose some National Health
leaflets . . .' and it goes on and on and on.

The Poem of the Week slot (10 quid prize)
helps boost a meagre salary – 'Content
of Telford, Mrs' wins most frequently,
or dour 'MacDonald (Mrs), Aberdeen'
('I'm really sure Our Lord and Billy Graham
Will put an end to all this horrid mayhem',
'To football hooglums' [sic] 'will come a day
When they repent that they have gone astray');
I chuck the other pratts straight in the bin –
hundreds of poor sad losers every week.

Creamy-pink curled tongues speckled with pollen dust:
slightly vanilla edge and the syrupy
　　　blend in the fumes of honeysuckle,
　　　　　cleanly, deliciously sweet, uncloying.

　This, and dusk fragrance of hay (most of the field has been
　　　　　　　　　　　　　　　　　　　cropped
mingle as, nosing the cru, we remark its generous finish.

Mixed mild and bitter – I thank you sir, kindly!
Haven't I been proper rotten with flu like?
Rotten with flu I been, all this week, I have.
Been in bed all the week, missed the old voting –
you know, the polling like, having the flu like.
Not as a vote off me'd make any change like.
Fixed they am, all the same, all the same them lot.
Once they gets Parlerment, hear no more of em.
This is it, this is it – speak as I find, me.
Speak as I find I does, all the same them lot.
Him as is standing's just same as them others.
End up no better off. Bitter and mild please.
I thank you kindly sir! You take old Churchill.
That was the feller as showed em all, Churchill.
That was the boy for the job was old Churchill.
That's what the country could do with now mister.
Industry, you know like, that's what we need like.
Soon be as dead as a yo-yo this country.
Ask me like, and I'd say dead as a yo-yo.
Soon be as dead as a yo-yo like, I'd say.
Still, that's the way as they wants it and that's the way as they'll get
it.

The tramp's scalp's indigo pus-oozing boil;
sulphur dioxide piss-hued cumulus;
a mac daubed with puked Chinese take-away –
drooled noodly detail of a Jackson Pollock;
furred upside-down tench in a mauve canal . . .
I sing the Grotty [no alternative].

'. . . terribly sad news . . . instantly . . . Motorway . . .'
After your mother's letter I turn to a
diary, through whose Wetmore Order
ornithological recollections

stir, of a friendship early-established and
special surviving global vicissitudes.
        Marvellous, those first close-shared eras
        mist-netting rarities, early migrants.

[Batty/unhealthy – verse at the best of times
chunters to insubstantial minorities,
        as for addressing lines to *dead men!*,
        arrogant therapy/piffle, claptrap.]

East and west coast observatories fêted us
(icterine and melodious warblers,
        thrill of *Phylloscopus bonelli*,
        magnified instants of bright crisp focus)

even as that sad realm in the middle was gently expiring
devenustated but yet, even though feculent, *ours*.

[Therapy, whining, anxious to demonstrate
how the nice bard is awfully sad about
        having his old pal flenched by crunched car –
        others' bereavements don't marvel readers.]

25 years ago, we, at a spring's brink, tasted a chilled draught;
        [Hippocrene hogwash] tonight, mawkish, I, solo, glut hock . . .

those days we charted our years by the dark swift coming and
                                                going . . .

                                        wants ⎫
[Who do you think you are whining to? No reader shares ⎭ your
                                                bereavement
and it's pathetic and mad to address yourself to the dead.]

Similar, thank you squire, bitter and mild mixed.
I thank you kindly sir! Same with them Irish
and them Iramians – that Ayertolly,
him with the whiskers like, look out for him mate.
Lunatic, he is mate, L-O-O – listen,
all the same, them lot are, mad on religion.
All them religerous lot is fernatics.
Stick all them bleeders together and let em
blow bloody buggery out of each other –
Prodestant, Catherlic, Jews Isleramics.
Whisky's no good to you mister I tell you,
Not when you're lying down, any road mister.
I been in bed for two days with the flu like,
any road, thought as I'd just have a whisky –
get me back on to me feet as they say like –
any road, straight to me kidneys it went like.
Straight to the kidneys – that's lying down, that is.
Standing's the thing like if you drinks the whisky,
by-pass the kidneys the whisky will then like.
Don't touch the kidneys at all then like, standing.
Never lie down if you're drinking the whisky.
All people got their own diffrent religions.
Obvious, that is like. Obvious, that is.
No need to kill all them others what aren't yours.
Them Sheeks with turbans on, thems just the same like.
Also them terrorists – see in the *Sun* where
that lot let off a bomb? Lunatics them mate –
L-U-N. Not to the kidneys, the *livers* –
straight to the livers and buggers em up mate.
Just half in there please squire. I thank you kindly!
All got the diffrent idees like, so we got to accept it.

The Buffet carriage lurches side to side
causing a democratic crocodile
(*Financial Timeses*, *Suns*, a *TES*,
spinsterly, oil-rig drunk, a see-through blouse,
two Sikhs, a briefcased First Class parvenu)
to jig like salts on storm-tossed quarterdecks.
They're queuing up to be insulted by
a truculent steward who administers
flabby cool BR toast at wondrous cost
and steaming tea in polystyrene cups
capped with thin leaky plastic lids – the car
oscillates and an old unfortunate
is scalded by spilt pekoe and then hurled
onto the carriage floor, striking her head
hard on an angle of formica counter.
A cooling tower, scrap cars bashed into cubes,
a preternaturally mauve canal.
The cut is dabbed with tissue, pronounced 'slight',
a volunteer fetches another cup,
someone produces an Elastoplast.
A Long Life shudders towards the table edge,
cramped buttocks stiffen in an orange scoop
of ergonomic fibreglass. Cropped boys
aged about sixteen, manifest recruits
(numbers and names and barracks stencilled white
on khaki kit bags), smoke, guffaw and swig.
One of their number, as a furious shepherd
might bellow some remonstrance at his dog
when it is five fields off, recalcitrant,
brays 'Ara sexy gerraknickersorf!'.
(A teenage girl of average composition,
buying a cling-filmed slice of currant cake,
stimulates this encomiastic greeting.)
Their left hands grip their right biceps, whereon
their right forearms are raised and lowered. One
pustular soldier of the Queen pretends
to grapple with an imaginary huge
phallus – his fellow-warriors are seized

with mirthful paroxysms. They all have spots
(compulsorily shaved, not left to heal)
and all read comics – caricature army,
balloons of speech exploding from the heads:
'Chuck me that Sten, I'll get the dirty dastards'.
Slight, acned raw cadets who may well be
spatchcocked in Ulster or some bloody fool
flag-waving bunkum like the Falklands do . . .
Company Sergeant Grit – Soldier of Stone,
Battling Burgess of the Fifty First,
Stens in the Jungle, 'Get me them grenades,
I'll show the ruddy rats how us Brits fight' . . .
The peaceful fields are littered with new lambs
fattening up for Easter, SO_2,
pretty canary-yellow against grey,
sweals from stark plant (the voguish acid rain),
Long Lifes vibrate, totter towards the edge.

Each time *Tornadoes* hedgehop the quarry head,
cleaving the brain-pan, tangible stridencies
judder a fossil bivalve free from
400 million years locked in matrix;

so I assumed it was these urbane killers caused the explosion
(sonic boom) but I was wrong – **TRACTOR TYRE BLOW-UP
KILLS YOUTH**.

The blushful Phillida hath been abroad –
limp 'coral' Nuform, body-shaped flat oats.

Generous Empire boldly was stencilled in
gold on a quart stone flagon converted for
    use as a bedside lamp in Gran's room.
        Dappling its girth was a painted world map

showing in red the bits that were under our
Sovereign's protection – much of the planet was
    cheerfully daubed thus, in those gone times;
        cruelty and mess, one assumed, reigned else-
            where.

Scion of large-eared risible Monarchy
serves now the useful negative function of
    non-doing but of being Royal
        thereby restricting all upstart PMs . . .

Obsolete heirloom, comforting glow of **Generous Empire**
    (cruelty and mess, I suppose, may be worse elsewhere than here).

or the sheer scale of these concepts (distance, time, structural elegance governing the basic particles of which you speak) in any way determine your philosophical – one might almost say theological – apprehensions?

No, I don't think so – certainly not the latter. If one contemplates a so-called Grand Unified Theory of Matter, it is a system of physical causes, rather than some kind of Reason with a capital R and the implicit mumbo-jumbo of all that, which one conceives –

You are quite happy, then, with a Reasonless universe?

Oh yes. Quite happy to accept Reasonless causal physics.

Tell us about your work with VLBI.

Yes, well, in Very Long Baseline Interferometry a number of astronomers, maybe around the world, examine a common radio emission simultaneously. They keep precise track of the timings with an atomic clock – extremely accurate, you know. The tapes of their radio observations are then flown to an HQ where they're played back exactly synchronized, and they're then joined electronically. The effect is like a giant connected radio telescope.

And you 'look' at, what?

Well, my only concern is with quasars but of course this covers a huge range of phenomena. 3C 273, for example, is the nearest one to this planet (2000 million light years). But it is with rather more distant subject-matter that I'm dealing. Until recently, we knew the so-called Double Quasar as the most distant (10 000 million light years) and my colleagues at the Very Large Array in New Mexico have produced very detailed radio pictures. But we're now aware of even more remote

Just half in there please squire. I thank you kindly!
Trouble is see what the trouble is see is
diffrent religions like. All of us know like
there must be *Something* like, you know Out There like.
This can't be all there is to it like. Course not.
You know like outer space, Some One or Some Thing
must have like made it like, must be a Reason.
This is a quote like so somebody *said* it:
'Man is a very religerous creature.'
Only they got Gods as isn't the same like,
so they starts killing the ones with the wrong Gods.
No sense in that mister, no sense in that mate.
Lunatics they are mate, L-U-N, all them
Arabs and Jews and them Christian Militias,
them Irish Paisleyists, dead simple mister,
all them old Shreeks with the turban like, all dead
simple mate, lunatics. Let it stand. Loonies.
That's Uman Natur mate, soon be as bleeding dead as the yo-yo.

Somewhere in *Far East* there was a *Narmistice*
(I wasn't sure where either of these things were);
wirelesses fizzled, grown-ups seemed to
value *it* more than they did my birthday! –

I was just 7 (July 27th, '53) and the
news there would be no more war made me feel comfy inside.

to say that aftermaths *occupy your attention mainly?*

Yes, insofar ·as one's foci are the radio galaxies, detectable as compact-radio-source quasars, which are the indications of after-math (in the centres of quasars, gas streams are spiralling into massive black holes). These central violent explosions throw out a couple of lobes stretching several million light years, so radio pictures show this as a kind of dumb-bell shaped emission.

Tell us about this particular one, will you?.

Yes, well, it's the remotest currently known. It's best discernible from the Parkes, Australian, radio telescope – indeed, was first picked up by that instrument. It was too remote, you know, and too far south to have been detectable by the Third Cambridge Survey, so doesn't feature in that catalogue – it was noted later in the Parkes survey. PKS 2000–330, it's classified as, and about 12 000 million light years from this planet, a

'Tell you what, old chap, *strictly* between ourselves,
I have a *leetle* personal whatsaname –
    utterly *vital* I drink daily,
        huge amounts, otherwise get so damn sad.'

. . . arrogant puny assumption that physics, uncomprehended,
must be the magic of some kind of Super-Mastermind Giant
[ham-philosophical sham-scientific atheist chunter].
Tantum religio potuit suadere malorum
(hideous Holies are hammering fuck out of other-believers).
Simple complexity, dying, euphoria, nastiness, good fun –
perfectly straightforward, no need to seek for variants of the
theisms sired by the earliest hominid terrified shamans
(cowardly greedy-weak graspings at seedy, trite consolations).
Tosh don't elucidate feeble inadequate cranial strivings.
Straightforward mystery; no need for transcendentalist hogwash.
Ave! no-nonsense astronomers probing Reasonless physics
    [also the modest who just cope with No Hope, without god].

       '54: old Miss Clio was teaching us
    all about *Frontiers* (Asia and everywhere);
       my mate's big brother, so he told me,
         'died in Career for one of those things' . . .

when he was in the bath, you could see scars on both of Dad's
                        shoulders
(carrying rails for Japan) – I hated flipping Frontiers.

Crozier, coiled crook, scroll of new-sprouting green
fern at a well's brink sprung from parched mountainside.
        Kneeling I sucked the silver fountain . . .
            [Tastefully Hippocrene, verbose gobful.

Prosaically between you and the summit, hacking, appeared a
    grizzled agrestic old get, wielding a bloody big scythe.]

Where my best mate lived, it was a scruffy dump
(mind you, the outside lav was a novelty),
        cockroaches scuttled – his mam called it
            'cockeroach', gaining an extra syll-thing.

Next door, the whippets shat in the scullery,
    bloke used to smack his wife with a dirty old
        hessian coal-sack, called her 'fuck-pig',
            got put in jail when their baby snuffed it.

What you should do was share out the money and
make some new houses so they'd be comfy and
        teach them to wash to stop their smell and
            show them what fun it was, being humans –

once you could teach them to dislike themselves as you did, then
                                                    clearly
    things'd be smashing of course – a child of 8 could see *that*.

I edit Readers Writes (the Letters page):
'What has gone wrong with Britain since the War?',
'Ex-Soldier, Telford' asks, 'The Socialists
allowed the lower orders too much hope
by promising them radically improved
living conditions, and the dangerous
doctrine of lower-class participation –
the riff-raff started meddling in Power . . .'
'I blame the Immigrants', 'Housewife' opines,
'for inner-city strifes . . .', 'The world's gone mad!',
'Sir – Are we to assume that Western Powers
exercise no control upon their own
Military Forces? Murder has been done;
but if it suits a Military Élite
(under a Government's auspices or not)
no felon may be charged – an impotent
electorate sees its Judicature abused
by its elected leadership . . .', 'I heard,
distinctly, on the 4th of January,
the Cuckoo calling in St. James's Park . . .'
Of course you can't print half of them – obscene
or batty: 'Mrs Thatcher is a cunt'
(plenty like that, whichever PM's in),
'I'd bomb the fucking wogs', 'Hanging's too good
for bastards like that' (muggers, hijackers,
people with beards, the unemployed, the child-
molesters, Hindus – everyone, it seems,
arouses someone's wrath), 'Dying's too good
for vermin like this' [so we stay alive].

A lady's album of 1826
in my possession, contains the following
pentameter one-liner unexplained:

This waiting bravely to be badly hurt.

[Untrue. *You* scrawl the whining metaphor
before the scalpel, can't now justify
expatiation. Call it a day at that.]

'Unemployed/Hopeless' doesn't sufficiently
serve to explain Cro-Magnon atrocities,
            vindicate *Homo troglodytes.*
            Dominant morphisms wield big cudgels.

'60: I bored my mates in the 4th Form by
forecasting martial law in the larger towns –
            Liverpool, Glasgow, London, Belfast,
            Birmingham – nobody thought I *meant* it!

You could see, in the estates and the new slum high-rises, Morlocks
sullenly honing rank fangs; telly-taught, butcherous, brute.

'Wearing a widow's tweeds I is any road,
stiplified NO FLOWERS at the funereal,
      weighed up the mows and cons I did like,
            "Better proceed with a caution" I says.'

Demented widow lives ten years in wardrobe
when hubby croaks; one-armed volcano victim
nurses mashed tot and yowls; for some shite god,
possession, border, tenet, goons blast cack
out of each other's chitterlings . . . I don't care
two fucks for any other pratt. UK's
OK. I'm lucky and intend to stay so.
What do you want, me to go batty too?

Pinions veed back a peregrine stooped out of
cumulus into 2000 *canutus*
      zigzagging silver over mudflats.
            Flurry of snowy down; slate-dark scythe wings

lugged the prey westerly, do you remember? [Do you remember?
Whom you address is now dead. Why yammer on to yourself?]

brutality ⎫
Strike out the old obsessive mortality ⎭ . . .
[Physics (unlike text) can't be corrected, though.
Let it stand. Ave! Age of Floored Proofs.
Stet (no alternative), leave as printed.]

Our land is no as bad as all that!
　　For when you watch TV
You see a lot of evil that
　　Is in many a foreign country.
For example you could take France
　　Who test the Atom Bomb
And lead a very merry dance
　　To every Harry, Dick and Tom
Who live on the islands where they test –
　　Old Frenchie kills them with the Fallout
And is, to the natives, a rare pest
　　And has driven them all out
Of their homes. And when they protest
　　(The Greenpeace with scruffy beard)
The French blow them up with the rest
　　And never a word
Is said against them. 'Tis a crime!
　　But that's only the Goverment,
Which ordinary folks, like yours and mine,
　　Can't control – perhaps they're sent
By Almighty God to try us
　　And the ordinary Frenchman is not cruel.
Och! let us all be pious
　　And no be sic a fool!

[£10 to you, Mrs McDonald, for your very good poem.]

Mirage of tangible air, heat-rippled pollened and sweet,
rises as if seen through gently vibrated cellophane, out of

pub garden well-tended beds. Blaze of a mid-day in June;
yeastily fragrant of new bread, a buff-frothed pint of bright amber,

cool on an oak table, gleams. (Inverse of Elegy, this.)
Collared doves double-moaning alarmed rise out of the road dust –

elderly woman and teenager boy (son? grandson? a nephew?)
slam the car doors and lock up, settle in yew-shaded chairs.

Briefly the boy disappears and a short time later returns with
two drinks – a cider for him, for his companion white wine.

Suddenly, right in the middle of platitudinous natter,
drips, magnified by her specs, ooze *Oh I miss him so much!*